Other Books by
R.L. STINE

SERIES:
- Goosebumps
- Fear Street
- Rotten School
- Mostly Ghostly

INDIVIDUAL TITLES:
- *It's the First Day of School…Forever!*
- *The Haunting Hour*
- *The Nightmare Hour*
- *Zombie Town*
- *The Adventures of Shrinkman*
- *The 13th Warning*
- *The Creatures from Beyond Beyond*
- *My Alien Parents*

THREE FACES OF ME

Text copyright © 2000 Parachute Press
Cover illustration by Tim Jacobus

A Parachute Press Book

Published by Amazon Publishing
P.O. Box 400818
Las Vegas, NV 89140

ISBN-13: 9781612183268
ISBN-10: 1612183263

R.L. STINE

THREE
FACES
OF ME

amazonpublishing

INTRODUCTION

• R.L. STINE •

"Ever think it might be nice to have two of you? You know, somehow magically split yourself into two people?"

That's how this book begins. And to tell you the truth, it's an actual thought I had one day. I was sitting at my desk, staring at my computer screen. The screen was blank because I hadn't written anything yet.

I was struggling with a new story idea. I just couldn't get it to work. I stared at the keyboard. Then I stared at the ceiling.

Then I had a thought: What if there were *two* of me. Wouldn't it be great to have a double?

R.L. Stine II could sit there and do my work. And I would go out and meet friends and go places and have a good time. When I came home, my writing would be done and I could take it easy.

It seemed like a simple idea. But I'm a big worrier. I started to worry about my double, R.L. Stine II.

Where would he sleep? What would he eat? The same food as me?

Would he have my mind? Would he have my memories? What would we talk about? Would we already know each other's thoughts?

What if my double went out on the street and people thought he was me? What if he went to see my friends and *pretended* he was me?

What if he decided to take over? What if he told everyone he was the original and I was R.L. Stine II?

You see, I worry a lot. And that's lucky— because my worrying helps me get the ideas for stories. And the more I thought about it, I decided the idea of having your own double would make a good, creepy book.

I'd written about doubles before. It's a subject I like a lot because I think it can be very scary.

I wrote a book in the Goosebumps 2000 series called *I Am Your Evil Twin*. In this book, a boy named Montgomery is sitting in school. He looks out the classroom window and sees someone staring in at him from outside. To his horror, he realizes the boy staring in at him is HIM.

Later, I wrote a book in the Nightmare Room series called *Liar Liar*. This book is about a boy named Ross, who likes to tell lies. Ross goes to a party—and who does he see across the crowded room? He sees *himself*.

Ross is terrified. He knows he doesn't have a twin. He's desperate to tell someone about his double. But no one will believe him. Why should they? He lies all the time. It turns out that Ross has lied so much, he's lied himself into another world.

I *hate* when that happens—don't you?

Anyway, I had the start of an idea for *Three Faces of Me.* I knew it would be about problems between a boy and his exact double.

But how would the boy—Ira Fishman—get his double? I started to think about cloning. When scientists clone, they take cells from an animal and use them in the birth of a new animal. The new animal is a double of the animal whose cells were used.

I learned about a woman who had a dog she really loved. The dog was getting old, and she knew he would soon die. But he was a very special dog. He was very smart. He could open doors and close them. He could open the refrigerator door and bring her a can of soda. He understood hundreds of words.

The woman took him to Korea where scientists have cloned dogs. It cost thousands of dollars. But soon there were five or six tiny puppies, all clones of her original dog. She took one home, and he was just as clever and smart as her dog.

I thought about cloning for this story. But it's too slow. I needed an *instant* way for Ira's double to appear. For some reason, the idea of a camera popped into my head.

Ever since the camera was invented there have been people who thought cameras were evil. Many people thought it was horrible luck to have your photo taken. They believed that the camera stole your spirit right out of your body.

From the time the camera was invented, people enjoyed doing scary things with them. Early photographers figured out clever ways to make *ghosts* appear in their photos. When people saw the weird images in the photos, they *believed* they were seeing real ghosts.

One of my most popular Goosebumps books was called *Say Cheese and Die!* In the book, some boys find a camera that takes pictures of horrible things that happen in the future. Every time they snap a photo, something *terrible* happens to one of them.

So, okay. Watch out for the camera in *Three Faces of Me.* Every time Ira clicks it, he's going to be in double trouble!

Hope you enjoy the book. Hope you read it TWICE!

RL Stine

CHAPTER 1

Ever think it might be nice to have two of you? You know, somehow magically split yourself into two people?

The other one of you could do all the chores, and keep your room neat, and argue with your little brother, and do all the homework.

And while he's doing that, you could be watching TV. Or playing ball outside with your friends. Or you could do the best thing of all—just goof off.

Doesn't that sound like a totally cool idea?

Well, you'd better be careful.

Thinking like that can get you into some pretty heavy trouble. Having a double can be a whole lot of fun—but it can also be really tricky.

How do I know?

Well, I guess I should begin at the beginning...

My name is Ira Fishman. Some kids call me Fish, but I don't mind. Fish is an awesome nickname.

Especially since I don't look like a fish or anything. I mean, I've never seen a fish with red hair and freckles!

The story begins when my eight-year-old brother, Zack, and I were walking home after school last Tuesday. Our house is only four blocks from school, so we always walk.

Every day we pass by the Corner Candy Shop. And every day we walk right by the game machine outside it. It's one of those glass machines with all sorts of little toys and stuffed animals inside.

You put a quarter in and move this big claw and try to pick up one of the toys in the claw and drop it down the chute so you can have it.

We pass by it every day. We don't stop because Zack and I never have any change.

But Tuesday afternoon I was lucky enough to find a quarter at the playground.

And guess what?

That's right.

We stopped at the machine and decided to see if we could win something.

I pulled the quarter out of my jeans pocket and dropped it into the slot. The machine started to hum and shake. I grabbed the control and started to move the claw.

I saw a squirt gun in there that looked pretty good. And some kind of model sports car.

I figured if I got a stuffed animal, I'd give it to Zack. I mean, what's an eleven-year-old going to do with a stuffed animal anyway? Right?

"Move it this way!" Zack cried. "No! That way! That way! No! Move it back!"

Big help, huh?

"Give me a break," I groaned.

The claw was tricky to move. When I pulled the control left, the claw went to the right. When I pushed up, the claw went down.

"You've got something, Ira! Close the claw! Close it!" Zack yelled.

I closed the claw and something slid down the chute.

Wow! I was practically shaking. I was pretty excited to win something on my first try.

But the prize didn't look too great.

It was a little black box made of plastic. I pulled off the clear wrapping and examined it.

"What is it?" Zack asked, grabbing for it. He was excited, too.

"I think it's some kind of camera," I said, holding it out of his reach. "I'm not sure where you put the film or anything. There aren't any instructions."

"Awesome. A camera!" Zack said. But I could tell he was disappointed. He wanted the squirt gun, too.

We made our way home and let ourselves into the house. Mom and Dad work in the same office. They both usually get home around five-thirty.

We took the little black box up to my room to examine it better. I kept rolling the camera around in my hand, trying to figure out how it worked.

I sat down at my desk and turned on the bright desk lamp. "How does it take pictures?" Zack asked, sticking his head in the way so I couldn't see the camera.

"I don't know," I told him, shoving him back. "I think this green thing is a button to push. But I don't see where you aim it."

"Can I have it?" he asked. He always wants everything I have, even if it's a piece of junk like this camera.

"No," I said. "I want it."

"I'm hungry," he said, in the whiny voice he uses when he doesn't get his way.

I pushed the little green button on the top of the box.

Nothing happened.

"Okay. Let's go downstairs and get a snack," I said. "I think I saw some cookies in the cabinet." I put the box on the desk, and we went down to the kitchen.

We finished all the chocolate chip cookies in the bag and drank some apple juice. Then Zack's friend

Marv came over. Zack and Marv went outside to play.

I fooled around for a while. Then I went back upstairs to start my homework.

Mrs. Quinn gives us tons of math problems to do every night. But I don't mind. I'm really good at math. Maybe I'm weird or something, but I really like doing math problems.

I started into my room, but then I stopped.

A boy was sitting at my desk. He had my math book open. He seemed to be doing math problems.

He had red hair and freckles. And he was wearing the same clothes as me.

My mouth dropped open. I stared at him really hard. He *was* me!

CHAPTER 2

I blinked and shook my head, but he didn't go away. I walked up to the desk. He looked just like me in every way.

He was even left-handed like me. And he held the pencil in the funny, slanted way I do.

He looked up. "Hi," he said, smiling. He sounded just like me. He smiled just like me.

I thought maybe I was looking into a mirror. Maybe he was just my reflection. Only my reflection was sitting—and I was standing.

"Who are you?" I asked.

"I'm Ira Fishman," he said.

I just stared at him. I couldn't talk. Finally I said, "No, I am."

"Slap me five," he said, just the way I always do. He held out his hand, and I slapped him five.

"You look just like me," I said. "But who are you really?"

"I told you," he said. "Ira Fishman."

"But that's me," I protested. My voice was getting high and whiny like Zack's.

"Me, too," he said calmly.

"You're me?" I cried.

"I guess."

"But if I'm me, how can you be me?"

He just shrugged, the way I shrug when I don't know the answer to something.

"I'm hungry," he said. "Could you run down to the kitchen and get me a snack?"

"Zack and I finished all the cookies," I told him.

"Do you have any apples?" he asked.

"Maybe," I said.

"Could you peel one for me?" He went back to the math problems.

"Listen, I don't know who you are, but you can't stay here," I told him. "Get out of my chair. You've got to go."

That didn't make him very happy. He bit his lower lip, just the way I do. "Go where?" he asked.

"I don't know."

"But I live here," he said. "This is where the Fishmans live, right?"

"Right," I said.

"Well, I'm Ira Fishman."

"But so am I," I said. This was getting me upset. I couldn't help it. You'd be upset, too, wouldn't you?

"I guess we're both Ira Fishman," he said.

"But I was Ira Fishman first," I told him. I had him there. He couldn't argue with that. I'm a very good arguer. Just ask my parents.

"Prove it," he said. He picked up the pencil and started doing more division problems.

"Put that down," I said, starting to get angry. "That's my homework."

"Mine, too," he said, concentrating really hard on a problem. "Help me with this one."

"That proves it!" I screamed. "That proves you're not me. Because I'm great at math. I never need help with the problems!"

He turned back to me. "Don't be a jerk," he said. "Look at me. If I'm not you, then who exactly am I?"

Score one for him.

I could see that he was a good arguer, too. "I don't care who you are!" I shouted.

I was really losing my temper now. "You can't stay here! What will Mom and Dad say? What will you eat? Where will you sleep?"

He pointed to my bunk bed across the room. "There's plenty of room," he said. "I'll take the bottom bunk. I don't like to sleep up high."

CHAPTER 3

We were still arguing about the bunk when I heard
Zack and Marv running up the steps. "Quick—
hide!" I whispered. "They'll see us both!"

My double didn't move from the desk chair.
"You hide," he said.

"You've got to go!" I whispered, shooing him
away with my hands. I was frantic.

"No way," he said, crossing his arms stubbornly.

Zack and Marv were on the landing now. In a
few seconds they'd be in the room and see both of
me. And how could I ever explain it?

I had no choice.

I dived behind the bed. Just in time. Zack and Marv came running in, all out of breath.

"Can I eat dinner at Marv's?" Zack asked my twin at the desk. I peeked out from behind the bed. Zack didn't notice that it wasn't really me.

"Is it okay with Marv's mom?" my double asked.

"I don't know. She isn't home yet," Marv said.

I saw Zack pick up the little black box from the desk.

No! I thought. *Don't press it, Zack. Don't press it!*

I had a pretty good hunch that the box was responsible for the fact that there were now two of me. What else could have done it?

Zack put the black box down. "Please," he whined, pulling my double's arm. "Please let me!"

"Well, wait till Marv's mom gets home," the double said. "If it's okay with her, I'm sure it'll be okay with our mom."

That seemed to satisfy the two boys. They turned and ran out of the room.

Zack had no idea that he was talking to a fake me. That gave me a very funny feeling in my stomach.

I had to get out and think this over. Whenever I have some hard thinking to do, I get on my bike and ride around and around the block as fast as I can. It always seems to help me think more clearly.

That's just what I had to do now.

I climbed out from behind the bunk bed. "I'm going outside," I told my double.

He looked disappointed. "Aren't you going to help me with the math?"

"No," I said. "You do it. And don't make any mistakes. I have a perfect average in math."

"Big deal," he said, making a face. The same face I always make.

I got out of there as fast as I could. I really wasn't feeling too well.

I rode around the block six or seven times. It felt good. And it helped me think.

When I put the bike back in the garage, I knew what I had to do.

Mom and Dad were home. I went running into the kitchen. They were peeling carrots, making a salad. They looked very surprised to see me come in the kitchen door.

"Oh. Did you go out?" Mom asked. "We thought you were still upstairs working on your math homework."

So they had been fooled by my double, too.

I took a deep breath. "I have to tell you something," I said. "That wasn't me upstairs. That was a second me. A fake. Something happened this afternoon, and now there are two mes."

They both laughed.

"Tell both of you to wash his hands," Dad said. "Dinner is in five minutes."

"I'm serious!" I said. "There are two of me now. The other one looks and sounds just like me."

"That's great," Mom said. "Now you can argue with yourself instead of arguing with us all the time."

They laughed again. They didn't believe me.

I decided I had to show them. I started to pull Mom by the arm. "Come with me. I'll show you," I said.

"Come on, Ira. Give us a break," Dad said. "We're trying to get dinner on the table."

"Please," I told them. "It'll only take a minute. Then you'll see there are two of me."

Finally, by begging and pleading, I got them to follow me upstairs. I put my finger to my lips and told them to be real quiet so we could sneak up on the other me and catch him by surprise.

We tiptoed up the stairs. Mom and Dad kept giving each other bewildered looks.

We didn't make a sound as we tiptoed into my room.

"I see him!" Mom said, pointing to the bed. "He's invisible, right? An invisible Ira? He looks just like you—only he's invisible!" She laughed at her own bad joke.

He wasn't there.

No one at the desk. The math book was closed. The notebook, too.

No one in the room.

"I don't get it, Ira," Dad said, shaking his head. "Aren't you a little old for imaginary friends?"

I felt like a real jerk.

Mom and Dad hurried back downstairs. I slumped down onto the lower bunk.

The closet door opened. The fake me stepped out. He had a big smile on his face. "What's for dinner?" he asked.

CHAPTER 4

What a terrible night! I was up for hours. I couldn't get to sleep.

That's because I was in the top bunk. I never sleep in the top bunk.

But you-know-who got to the bottom bunk first.

He also got down to dinner first. He locked me in my room. Then he went down and ate my food. I could hear everyone talking and laughing down there. No one knew that it wasn't the real me having dinner with them.

Later, after everyone had gone to bed, I sneaked down and got some cold chicken from the refrigerator. I was starving!

When I got back upstairs, my double was sound asleep in the bottom bunk. I climbed up to the top and tried to think of what I should do.

I thought about it a long time. And I decided that having a double might not be so bad. In fact, having a double could be a great thing!

When the alarm clock rang at seven the next morning, I hopped down from the bunk and shook my double awake.

"Huh? What's going on?" he asked.

"Wake up," I said. "You're going to school today. Come on. Hurry."

He yawned. "Why me? What are you going to do today?"

I gave him a big smile. "I'm going to stay home and have some fun," I said. "Maybe I'll stay in bed all day and read comic books."

I pulled him out of bed. I tossed him a red T-shirt and my jeans. He got dressed slowly. It took him a long time to wake up. Just like me.

"Ira—help me get dressed!" Zack was shouting from his room.

"Go help Zack," I told the double. He headed toward Zack's room.

I climbed back into bed. This was going to be awesome! My double could do all the work. I would have fun all the time.

I heard him in Zack's room, arguing about socks. Zack argued about what socks he was going to wear every morning. He never liked any of his socks.

I smiled. I didn't have to argue with him this morning.

I heard them go down to breakfast. I heard Dad yelling at them to finish their poached eggs. I smiled again. No yucky poached eggs for me.

After they leave, I'll have candy for breakfast, I told myself.

I planned my day. Comic book reading all morning. TV watching all afternoon.

A short while later I heard the front door slam. Everyone had left. I thought I'd be happy to be all alone in the house now. But I wasn't. I started thinking about how my double would get along in school.

Would he know which class was Mrs. Quinn's? Would he know what seat to sit in? Would he know who my friends were?

Maybe I should go check on him, I thought. Maybe I should make sure he knows what he's doing. Then I can come back home and have fun all day.

I jumped into some clothes, grabbed a candy bar for breakfast, and ran all the way to school.

Then I darted through the halls to Mrs. Quinn's class. The bell had already rung.

I poked my head in the door.

There he was, sitting in my seat. He was joking around with Scotty Furman, just the way I did every morning.

Mrs. Quinn turned her back to write something on the chalkboard.

I dashed in through the door at the back of the room and hid inside the supply closet. I pulled the door shut just as she turned around to begin class.

A few minutes later she started going over the math assignment. I heard her call me to the board to do the first problem.

I opened the closet door a tiny crack and peeked out. There was my double writing rapidly on the chalkboard.

I opened the door a little wider to see what he was writing. "Oh, no!" I gasped. I clapped a hand over my mouth. I hoped no one had heard me. But I couldn't help myself.

He was doing the problem *wrong!*

CHAPTER 5

It was a very bad morning.

My double missed two math problems and said some very dumb things during class discussion. Everyone laughed at him. I even saw Mrs. Quinn chuckling—but at least she tried to hide it.

At recess I ran out and hid behind a tree so I could watch him.

Oh no! Why is he playing with the girls? I wondered. What does he think he's doing?

I tried to wave to him to go play softball. I always play softball at recess. It's my favorite sport.

But he couldn't see me.

How embarrassing!

There he was, hanging around with the girls instead. What were my friends going to think?

Finally he wandered over to the softball game. That's more like it! I thought.

But I was wrong. He came to bat three times—and each time was an absolute disaster. "This can't be happening!" I cried, watching him strike out for the third time in a row.

"Way to go, Fish! Way to go!"

"Want to borrow my glasses, Fish?"

Everyone was laughing and carrying on. They all knew that I never strike out. Ever.

I pounded my fist against the tree trunk. I was never so embarrassed in all my life.

After school I watched him pack up my book-bag and head for home. I stayed around school for a while and talked to my friends.

I guess I was kind of lonely. I'd been hiding by myself all day.

By the time I got home, I was really angry. I knew I could never send my double to school for me again. I was much better at being myself than he was.

All he did was embarrass me.

I found him in the den. He was lying on the couch watching cartoons.

That made me even madder. I never watch cartoons after school. I always watch MTV.

"Hi," he said, smiling at me from his seat on the couch. "Did you have a nice day at home?"

"No, I didn't," I growled. I angrily clicked off the TV. "You didn't do a good job of being me at all," I told him. "I've had enough of you. I want you to leave—now."

"Huh?" He gaped at me.

I went over and started to pull him up from the couch.

"I'm not leaving," he said, and he pulled back. Since he was built just like me, he was as strong as I was.

"Don't make me mad, Ira," I said.

"Don't make *me* mad, Ira," he said.

"You can't live here," I shouted.

"But I do live here!" he shouted back.

I grabbed him and he grabbed me. This time I pulled him as hard as I could and yanked him off the couch. We started wrestling around on the floor.

Do you have any idea how weird it is to fight with yourself? We both kept trying to pin each other with the same moves.

Suddenly I had an idea. I let go of him and jumped up.

"You give up fast," he said, laughing.

"I haven't given up. I've won!" I cried.

I ran upstairs. I grabbed the black box off the desk. I hurried to bring it back down to the den.

"What are you going to do with that?" my double asked. He looked a little worried.

"I'm going to press the green button again," I said.

"No. Don't," he said. He looked a little more worried.

That made me smile. My idea must be right, I thought.

"I think if I press the button a second time, you will disappear," I said.

"No. Please." He looked *very* worried. "You don't want to do that!"

He tried to pull the little box from my hand. "I'm warning you. Don't push it."

"Goodbye," I said.

I pushed the green button.

CHAPTER 6

Nothing happened.

My double didn't move. And he didn't disappear.

I ran out of the den and out the kitchen door.

"Ira! Ira! Come back!"

He called after me, but I didn't care. I had to get out of there. I had to think.

"Ira! Hey—Ira!"

I ignored his shouts. I jumped on my bike and started pedaling as fast as I could.

Faster…Faster…

I like that feeling when you go so fast the ground becomes a blur. It really helps me concentrate.

I rode around and around the block, going as fast as I could. I was thinking hard. But I wasn't coming up with any answers to my twin problem.

Maybe I should try telling Mom and Dad again, I thought. If they actually saw my double, they'd believe me. Then they'd have to do something about him.

Maybe they could figure out how to make him disappear. Or maybe they could chase him away. Or get him adopted by some nice family.

Or maybe they'd decide we should keep him.

He could have the guest room. It might be nice to have a twin brother. There would always be someone to talk to and share ideas with.

I mean, he was a pretty good guy. After all, he was just like me.

But what would my friends think?

And could Mom and Dad afford another kid? They'd have to buy him his own clothes. He couldn't keep borrowing mine.

I pedaled faster. The ground went by in a blur. My thoughts were just a blur, too. A crazy, jumbled blur.

I wasn't paying any attention to where I was riding. I knew I was several blocks from home, but I just kept on going.

Suddenly, in front of a house up ahead, I saw a guy I knew from school. It was Andy Brooks. He was throwing a ball up onto his roof and then catching it when it rolled down.

"Hey, Andy!" I called.

But then I saw something that made me jam on the brakes. My bike skidded to a stop on the sidewalk.

I jumped off the bike and stared. I thought maybe my eyes were playing tricks on me. But they weren't.

There were two Andys playing ball against the front of his house!

CHAPTER 7

But of course there were two of them.

I was so worried and upset about my double that I wasn't thinking clearly.

Andy Brooks was a twin.

An identical twin.

Andy and Randy always played ball together. They did everything together. I mean, I never saw them apart. They were very close—even for twins.

"Nice brakes, Fish," Andy called to me. "Now why don't you try the horn?"

I looked down. I had stopped so fast, I had left black tire marks on the sidewalk.

"I...uh...I was just surprised to see you guys," I said.

I let the bike drop to the grass and jogged across their front lawn. "How's it goin'?"

"Okay," they both answered at once. Randy turned his back to me and tossed the ball up onto the roof.

He and Andy look exactly alike. They're both really skinny with blond hair, very pale skin, and dark blue eyes. But I knew it was Randy and not Andy.

How did I know?

Randy always wears red. When the twins were little babies, their parents kept track of which was which by always dressing Randy in red. And he was still wearing red even now.

The ball bounced over the gray roof shingles, then started to roll down. Randy made a nifty one-handed catch. Then he tossed the ball to me.

It was an old tennis ball. All of the fuzz had rubbed off. I tossed the ball up, but I threw it a little too hard. It bounced high on the roof, then sailed over to the other side, down into the backyard.

"Hey, way to go, Fish," Andy said sarcastically.

"Go chase it," Randy said.

All three of us ran to the back to look for it. We looked everywhere.

There was a big garden in back, and we looked under every flower and inside all the bushes and behind the trees, but we couldn't find the ball anywhere.

"Thanks for losing the ball," Andy grumbled.

"Yeah. Nice move, Ace," Randy said.

"What's it like to be twins?" I asked. The question just popped out of my mouth.

"What?" They both looked surprised.

"Really. What's it like to be twins?" I repeated. "Do you guys like it?"

"Do we have a choice?" Andy said. He was always sarcastic like that.

"It's pretty good," Randy said, still looking for the tennis ball.

"Yeah. One good thing is, you always have someone to play ball with," Andy said. And then he grumpily added, "If you *have* a ball, that is."

"And there's always someone to talk to late at night when you're supposed to be going to sleep," Randy said. "That's pretty great."

"And you can borrow the other one's clothes," Andy added. "And you can do your homework together. And there's always someone around to play video games with. And—"

"And sometimes you can play great tricks on people," Randy interrupted.

Andy laughed.

"What kind of tricks?" I asked.

"Well, once I went to Randy's class and he went to mine—for a whole day," Andy said.

"That's pretty cool," I agreed.

Maybe having two of me wouldn't be so bad after all, I was thinking. Randy and Andy seemed to have a great time with each other. Maybe my double and I could be just like them.

Maybe we'd be real pals.

"Trading classes wasn't cool at all," Randy said. "He got me into trouble and I had to stay after school and miss baseball practice."

"It wasn't my fault," Andy insisted.

"Oh, yeah? Then whose fault was it?"

"It wasn't me who was talking in class. Mrs. Quinn just *thought* it was me."

Randy picked up a pebble from the grass and tossed it at the side of the garage. It made a loud *thwack* and bounced away. "He's always getting me in trouble," he muttered, shaking his head.

"And he's always borrowing my stuff and ruining it," Andy complained. "He got my baseball glove soaking wet, and the leather stretched."

"It was an accident!" Randy shouted. "You know it was. But you just like to pick on me and give me a hard time."

He turned to me. "He's always picking on me, always bugging me. He always butts in when I'm on the phone. He thinks all of my friends have to be his friends, too."

"Do not!" Andy shouted. His face was bright red. "That is *so* not true!"

"He borrows my stuff and never returns it. He messes up our room, and I always get blamed for it. He's a total pig. He eats his dessert and then mine, too."

"I do not!" Andy was getting really angry.

"He copies off my homework. He's always bugging me to help him. I never get to be by myself. I always have to see him staring back at me twenty-four hours a day. I never get any privacy."

"That's not true!" Andy screamed. Both of their faces were bright red now. "You're a stupid liar!"

"He always calls me names, and then when I do it back—"

Randy didn't finish what he was saying. Andy had found the tennis ball in the grass. He picked it up and heaved it with all his strength at Randy.

The ball hit Randy right in the stomach. He cried out and then jumped at Andy.

"You want to fight?" He took a swing at Andy, but Andy ducked away.

They grabbed each other by the shoulders and began shoving each other around. Randy toppled over backward onto the grass. Andy jumped on top of him, and they began wrestling, rolling over and over, yelling, calling each other names.

"Hey, guys," I shouted. "Come on. Take it easy. Lighten up, okay?"

But they didn't hear me. They were both screaming at the top of their lungs, punching with both fists, really letting each other have it. It was not a very pretty sight.

"I guess you two answered my question," I said. But they didn't hear that, either.

I knew their fight would be over soon, and they'd be friends again. But I didn't feel like waiting around.

I walked quickly around to the front, picked up my bike, and rode off.

CHAPTER 8

The double *had* to go.

I didn't want to spend my whole life wrestling around on the ground. I didn't want someone else staring back at me all day, following me around, talking to all my friends, borrowing all my stuff.

I already had Zack to do all those things!

I pedaled back toward home, thinking hard, thinking of how to get my double out of the house, how to get the guy out of my life—for good.

"Whoa—!"

I suddenly remembered something.

I remembered the first time I pushed the button on the little black box. Nothing had happened.

Nothing.

I was disappointed. I put it down on my desk and went downstairs to get Zack and myself a snack.

And when I came back upstairs…there was the double sitting in my room.

Yes! Yes!

I realized I had just remembered something very important.

It took a little while for the box to work.

It didn't work immediately.

So this afternoon maybe I had run out of the house too soon. Maybe when I pressed the button a second time to make my double disappear…maybe it just took a minute or so for the camera to work.

Maybe he was already gone for good.

Maybe he disappeared a few minutes after I ran out of the house.

I pedaled for home as fast as I could. This thought really cheered me up. I had to be right.

I *had* to!

My problem was over. My life could go back to normal.

I zoomed up the driveway, jumped off my bike, and let it crash to the ground.

I dashed into the house, letting the screen door slam behind me. I checked the den first.

No one there.

Then I checked the living room. No one.

Yes! Yes! I pumped my fists in the air.

I was right! I was so happy.

I ran upstairs. I burst into my room.

"Hi," said my double. He was sitting on the lower bunk.

"Hi," said another double. He was sitting at my desk.

Now there were *two* of them!

CHAPTER 9

"I warned you not to press the button," my first double said. He was wearing exactly what I was wearing—a dark gray T-shirt and blue jeans. So was the second double.

I just stood and stared at them. You'd stare, too, if there were two other yous in your room!

"Hey, guy—I'm Ira Fishman," the new double said to me. "Slap me five."

"I know," I said gloomily. I slapped him five, but my heart wasn't in it.

"Nice to meet you, Ira," the new double said.

"Nice to meet you, Ira," I muttered.

"Where's he going to sleep?" I asked myself out loud. "There's no room for three of us!"

They went back to the talk they were having before I burst into the room. "What kind of cereal do you like?" my first double asked.

"CocoPops," my second double said.

"Me, too!" cried the first double. "What's your favorite sport?"

"I like baseball," answered the second double.

"I do, too!" cried the first double. He looked up at me. "Isn't this amazing? He's just like us."

"Amazing," I muttered.

"What's your favorite flavor bubble gum?" the second double asked.

"Banana," answered the first double.

"Mine, too!" cried the second double.

"Who's your favorite singer?" I asked.

"CC Mawl," they both answered.

"Mine, too!" I said.

They were such nice guys, it was hard to stay out of the conversation. But then I heard the front door slam downstairs.

"What's your favorite color?" my second double asked.

"Ssshhhhh," I told them both, waving frantically for them to shut up.

"Hey, Ira! Ira!" Zack was home. He was calling me from the bottom of the stairs.

"Blue," my first double answered.

"Mine, too! Amazing!"

"Shut up," I told them. Then I yelled, "I'm coming, Zack!" and ran out of the room just in time. Zack was hurrying up the stairs. "No. Stay down. Stay down," I told him. "I'm coming down."

Zack gave me a funny look as I pushed him backward down the stairs. "I'm starving," he whined.

"I'll fix you a sandwich," I said.

"Peanut butter and jelly," he said, still whining.

"I know. That's the only sandwich you eat."

I made Zack a sandwich, and I made one for me. Zack complained that I put too much jelly on his. He can be a real pain sometimes.

He kept complaining about it, but I didn't really listen. I was thinking about the two Iras up in my room. How was I going to keep anyone from seeing them? How was I going to get rid of them?

Zack finished his sandwich and went outside to see if Marv was around. I was too tired to get back on my bike and ride around the block again. So I flopped down on the couch in the den and tried to think.

But thinking on a couch isn't the same as thinking on a bike. I had no ideas. I decided to go upstairs and ask them what they thought. They were as smart as me. Maybe they'd have a good idea about what we should do.

I ran up the stairs two at a time and hurried into my room.

They were gone.

"Great!" I told myself. "Maybe they left together."

But then I heard voices coming from outside. The voices sounded like my voice.

I ran over to the window and looked down on the backyard. There were my doubles playing catch with a softball.

And there was Zack watching them from the driveway, a very confused look on his face.

CHAPTER 10

"Oh wow," I muttered. "Oh, wow. Oh, wow."

I stood frozen at the window.

I couldn't move. I couldn't think straight.

What was I going to do?

How could I explain this to Zack?

If I told him the truth, he'd probably get really scared.

I ran down the stairs just as Zack was coming in the back door. He still looked confused. And when he saw me in the house, he looked even more confused.

"How'd you get in so fast?" he asked. "I saw you in the backyard."

"I took a shortcut," I told him.

"But you were playing catch with yourself," he said. "There were two of you."

"What?" I acted surprised. "What on earth are you talking about, Zack?"

"There were two of you," he repeated. He looked at me as if I were playing some kind of trick on him. He scratched his head. "I saw you both," he said.

"Uh-oh," I said. "I'm a little worried about your eyes, Zack. I think you've got a problem."

"What do you mean?" he asked.

"Maybe you need glasses."

"No, I don't," he protested, crossing his arms in front of his chest.

"Well, if you're seeing double, you might need glasses," I said. "Let me give you a little test."

He thought about it for a while. "Okay," he said finally. "What kind of test?"

I held up two fingers. "How many fingers do you see?" I asked him.

He squinted hard at my raised fingers, raising one eyebrow, then the other.

"Two," he answered finally.

"Uh-oh," I said, shaking my head. "Two? Are you sure? Look again, Zack."

"I see two," he said.

"I'm only holding up one," I told him.

Then I held up four fingers. "Now how many do you see?" I asked him.

He squinted at my fingers. He took a long time. "Four," he answered.

"No. I'm only holding up two," I told him.

The poor kid looked like he might cry. I felt bad about playing a mean trick on him. I didn't like to lie to him. But what choice did I have?

"You—you really think I need glasses?" he asked in a tiny voice.

"Maybe, maybe not," I said. "Why don't you go lie down in the den and watch TV for a while. If you don't see double when you watch TV, you won't need glasses."

That idea seemed to cheer him up. He walked obediently into the den, and a few seconds later I heard the TV go on. "What are you watching?" I called to him.

"*Double Trouble*," he called back.

I had to laugh. That was kind of funny.

That dumb old show reminded me of my double trouble—those two troublemakers playing catch outside where anyone who walked by could see them.

I hurried to the back door. "Hey, guys! Hey! Ira! We have to talk!" I called.

No reply.

I stepped out and looked around.

"Ohhhh." I let out a low groan.

My heart sank to my knees.

They were both gone.

CHAPTER 11

Where did they go?

I was in a total panic. I had to bring them back before anyone saw them.

I took a deep breath and forced myself to calm down. I had to think clearly.

Where did they go? Where did they go? Since they're me, they would go where I would go, right? I reasoned. So—where would I go?

Hmmmm...I might go over to my friend Mark's house, I thought. Yes. There's a good chance I'd go to Mark's house and ask him if he wanted to play ball at the playground behind school.

I decided it was worth a try. I got on my bike and started pedaling like crazy to Mark's house.

It was just up the hill a few blocks away. But I felt like I was climbing a mountain. My legs were tired from all my earlier bike riding.

But it didn't matter. I knew I had to find the other Iras no matter what.

I was so angry. What did they think they were doing?

Did they really think they could both parade around together all over the neighborhood? Did they *really think* no one would notice that there were two of them?

They were so dumb! I would never do anything that dumb.

I finally got to Mark's house. I rode up his front walk, climbed off the bike, and rang his doorbell. I waited a minute, then I put my face up to the screen door. I could see Mark inside hurrying to answer the bell.

"Hey, Fish!" He looked really surprised. He stared at me from the other side of the screen door. "What are you doing back? I told you I can't play ball. My mom says I've got to watch my little sister this afternoon."

So I was right! They had been here. I was on the right trail.

"Oh. I...uh...I left my bike here. So I...uh... came back for it," I said. It was a pretty lame excuse. But it was the best I could do.

"But you—you weren't riding your bike," Mark said. He was looking at me like he didn't believe me.

"Oh. I guess you're right," I said. I jumped onto the bike, turned, and rode off as fast as I could.

CHAPTER 12

I turned the corner and headed for the playground. Passing the Corner Candy Shop, I suddenly realized I was starving.

I knew that I needed a Butter Bliss candy bar immediately. It would give me the energy I needed to find those stupid guys and drag them home.

Did I have any money?

I kept one hand on the bike's handlebars and reached the other hand deep into my jeans pocket.

Yes. I had a dollar bill.

I was supposed to give it to Mrs. Quinn to pay for a class field trip, but I had forgotten.

Excellent!

With a whole dollar I could buy two Butter Bliss bars.

I leaned my bike against the game machine—the machine that had caused me all of this trouble—and walked inside.

My mouth was watering. I could taste those creamy Butter Bliss bars already!

"You're back?" the man behind the counter said. He was very short and very bald, and he looked very surprised to see me.

"Excuse me?" I cried.

"You came back to pay me the money?"

Uh-oh. I knew I was in trouble.

"What money?" I asked.

"The money you owe me for those two Butter Bliss bars you bought a few minutes ago. You said you'd come right back, remember?"

"Oh. Yeah. Sure," I said. "Here I am."

"And the money?" He reached a big pink hand over the counter.

"Here," I said. I handed him the dollar bill.

He stuffed it quickly into his cash register. "Thanks a lot. I like an honest kid. You want anything else?"

"Well..." I said, trying to get the nerve to ask. "Could I maybe have one more Butter Bliss bar? I'll pay you for it tomorrow."

He gave me a strange look. "I'm all out. You took the last two when you were in here the first time—remember?"

"Oh. Right," I said. "I thought maybe you got a new shipment in."

"A new shipment in five minutes?"

I said goodbye and unhappily walked back out. Now I was really steamed.

My doubles had taken the last two Butter Bliss bars—and I had to pay for them! That wasn't fair.

At least they had been smart enough to send only one of them into the store. But that didn't make me feel any better.

I was tired. And starving.

And totally fed up with them.

When I finally got to the playground, I couldn't believe what I saw. There they were, near the volleyball nets, playing catch with my softball.

And not far away on the diamond, a softball game was going on with a lot of kids from my class. My doubles were right out in the open field. Both of them.

They didn't seem to care if anyone saw them!

I rode my bike across the grass as fast as I could. "Come on. Let's go!" I shouted. "We've got to get home."

They both smiled as if they were happy to see me. "Go home? Why?" one of them asked.

"We have to have a little talk," I said. "Come *on!*"

I think they could tell by the look on my face that I meant business. Pedaling slowly, I led my doubles away from the diamond, away from all the kids. I just wanted to get them home without anyone seeing them.

We almost made it.

We were at the far end of the playground, about to cross the street, when I heard somebody shouting. "Ira! Hey—Ira!"

I turned around, and there was Scotty Furman running toward us.

"Hey, Fish—wait up!"

It was too late to make a run for it. He saw all three of us. And he looked very upset and confused.

CHAPTER 13

No one said anything.

Scotty stood there staring at the three of us. The three of us stood there staring back at Scotty.

Finally I said, "Scotty, have you met my cousins?"

"Cousins?" By this time his eyes were practically bugging right out of his head. "Cousins? You're kidding—right! They look just like you!"

"Yeah," I said, trying to seem calm. "We're a very close family."

I started to lead my two doubles quickly across the street, but Scotty followed. "But—but you're dressed exactly alike!" he cried.

"Isn't that amazing?" I said. "We couldn't believe it, either. Just one of those weird coincidences!"

"Hey, guys!" Scotty called to the kids on the softball diamond. "Come here. You've gotta see this!"

"We have to go. We're late," I said.

"Hey—come over here! Look at Fish's cousins!" Scotty yelled.

About a dozen kids came running over the grass to see what the fuss was.

I jumped on my bike and pedaled full speed across the street. "Let's go!" I yelled to me and me.

The three of us took off.

"Hey, come back!"

"Fish—what's your hurry!"

"Hey, you guys! Come back here!"

Shouting, the kids chased after us, with Scotty in the lead. We turned the corner and started racing downhill. They were right behind us, yelling for us to stop.

No way.

No way we were going to stop.

One of the nice things about having three of you is that you can split up and run in three different directions. Which is just what we did.

One double turned left, one turned right, and I kept going straight.

The kids chasing us split up, too. But now they were totally confused.

And since they weren't really sure why they were chasing us in the first place, they gave up pretty fast.

I rode all the way home without looking back once. All three of us arrived at the back door at the same time. We were hot and sweaty and breathing hard.

"Okay, Ira and Ira, up to my room," I ordered.

"Why? What's going to happen?" one of them asked.

I frowned at them. "We're going to settle this problem once and for all."

CHAPTER 14

The two doubles plopped down on the rug in my
room and rested. I was too upset and angry to rest.
I paced back and forth in front of them.

"We've got to talk," I said.

I picked up the little black box from my desk. I
held it tightly in my hand, and I made sure my fingers were nowhere near the green button.

"When is dinner?" one double asked.

"When Mom and Dad get home," the other
double told him.

"Don't call them Mom and Dad," I snapped. "They're not your mom and dad—they're *mine*."

"Mine, too," the first double insisted.

"Mine, too," the other double said.

"Ugh!" I slapped my forehead with my hand.

"We're all Ira Fishman, right?" the first double remarked. "So we have to have the same mom and dad."

"Listen, guys," I started again. "This isn't working. We can't all be Ira Fishman and you know it."

"But we *are* Ira Fishman," the second double said.

"Look at us," said the first double. "Who else could we be? We're Ira Fishman. That's for sure."

"But, the three of us can't live together in this house," I argued. "It's too crowded."

"It was fine till you showed up," the second double said to me.

"But I was first!" I shouted.

"Are you sure?" he asked. "Are you *sure* you were first? Because actually, I think was first."

"No. I was first," the other double said, shaking his head. "I know it."

"Stop this! Stop it!" I was really losing my temper.

"Hey, I warned you not to press the green button," the first double said. "You didn't listen."

I held up the little black box. They looked surprised. They didn't know I had picked it up.

"There must be a way to reverse this," I said, rolling the box over and over, looking at it as carefully as I could. "There's got to be a way to make the two of you disappear."

The first double grabbed the box from my hand. "No way!" he said.

I grabbed for it. He tossed it to the second double.

I went after the second double. "Give that back!"

He tossed it over my head to the first double.

"Come on—give it to me! It's mine!" I shouted.

The first double swung around me and threw the box to the second double. They were having a great time playing keep-away.

But now I was really frightened.

What if one of them pushed the button on the little camera?

Would I disappear?

Or would another Ira Fishman show up instead?

This wasn't fair. It wasn't fair for them to barge into my house and try to steal my life!

"Whoooooah!"

With a loud groan, I jumped up and almost got the box.

But the first double caught it and tossed it back to the other double.

With a desperate dive, I lunged across the floor—and tackled the second double.

"Hey—!" he let out a startled cry. And as he went down, he tossed the camera to the first double.

Breathing hard, I climbed to my feet and leaped at the first double.

He fell back over the desk chair.

The chair crashed into the desk, knocking the desk lamp to the floor. It fell with a loud crash, shattering the lightbulb into a million shards of glass.

The double leaped over the glass and with a cry, he heaved the box toward the second double.

He threw too hard. The box sailed over the double's head and crashed against the bedroom wall.

He and I both dived across the room for it.

I got there first.

My whole body trembling, I picked it up—and dodged away as he tried to grab it from me.

I held it away from him. Held it to my eyes and studied it.

A small compartment had popped open.

I guess it happened when the box hit the wall.

And inside the small compartment—I saw a red button.

Green for go. Red for stop! I told myself.

"No!" both doubles cried at once. At the same time, the Iras made a desperate leap for the box.

I jerked it away from them—just as Mom poked her head into the room.

"What on earth is going on in here?" she cried.

CHAPTER 15

I pressed the red button.

The two other mes disappeared.

Vanished.

Mom blinked a few times and shook her head. "Why are you making such a racket, Ira? It sounded like there was an army up here!"

"Sorry, Mom," I said. "I was—you know—just fooling around." I shrugged the way I always do.

"It was just *you* making all that noise? I thought the house was falling in."

"Just me," I said. "Sorry."

I looked around the room. It was just me. Just one me.

Just one Ira Fishman. Not two. Or three. I was alone in my room.

Suddenly the room felt enormous. And I was so happy, I could burst!

"Are you sure you're feeling okay?" Mom walked over and felt my head. "Hmmm...feels normal," she said. "What's that?"

She was pointing to the little black box which I still gripped tightly in my hand.

"Uh...some kind of camera," I told her. "I don't think it works."

"Well, go wash your hands and come down for dinner," she said. "And that's enough goofing around for tonight, do you understand me?"

"Right," I said. "No problem."

As soon as she left, I leaped up in the air for joy. "No problem! No problem!" I shouted over and over.

My problems had disappeared. With the click of a button!

"Now, where can I hide you?" I asked the camera.

I bent down, pulled open my bottom desk drawer, and hid the little black box way in the back. I didn't want Zack or anyone else to find it and maybe push the green button by mistake.

That night I slept in the lower bunk again, all by myself. The next morning I had my breakfast and walked with Zack to school. I sat in my own seat in class, and I got all the math problems that were on the board right.

During recess, I played softball—and I hit a single and a home run. I fouled out once, but I didn't care.

I was happier than I'd ever been. It felt so good to be one person.

It was so nice not to look across a room and see myself staring back at me.

Once again I was me. The one and only me!

Then on Saturday morning Mom came up to my room and pulled all of my dressiest clothes from my dresser. "What's that for?" I asked suspiciously.

"I want you to look nice," she said. "We're spending the day at Aunt Melba's."

I groaned. "Oh, no."

"Stop that," Mom scolded. "Aunt Melba isn't so bad."

Oh, yes she is, I thought. Aunt Melba is the pits.

She pinches Zack and me till our cheeks are red and sore. Then she hugs us till our ribs crack. And she always smells like mothballs.

She cooks us the greasiest, heaviest, grossest food. And forces us to eat more and more. We always get sick from her food.

The last time we were there, she made Zack and me clean her filthy basement. Then she complained that we didn't do a good job.

Every time we visit Aunt Melba, she gets into a horrible fight with my dad. And she even has a dog that bites!

"Do we have to go?" I asked mournfully.

"Don't act like that," Mom said. "I know she isn't much fun. But she's your only aunt. Now hurry up. We're already late."

I groaned again. Mom went downstairs.

I pulled on my fancy, pleated khakis and my bright yellow buttondown shirt. What a shame. A perfectly beautiful Saturday ruined.

"Come on, Ira," Dad called from downstairs. "Zack's already dressed."

I slumped down the stairs. "You know how moody Aunt Melba gets if we're late," Mom said, straightening her skirt.

"Or if we're early," I muttered sadly.

We started out the front door. "Oh. Wait a minute," I said. "I forgot something." I turned and started back up the stairs.

"We'll be in the car," Dad called after me. "Just slam the front door behind you."

"Okay," I called back.

I ran into my room, got down on the floor, and pulled open my bottom desk drawer. Then I reached way to the back and pulled out the little black box.

I stood up—and pressed the green button.

Then I waited.

A few seconds later a double appeared. He was wearing the same fancy, pleated khakis and the same stiff yellow buttondown shirt as me.

"Hi," he said. "I'm Ira Fishman."

"I know," I said, giving him a big grin.

"Slap me five," he said, holding out his hand.

"We don't have time," I told him. "You're going to Aunt Melba's."

"I am?" He suddenly looked very unhappy.

"Get going," I said, giving him a little push. "You're late. They're waiting for you in the car. Just slam the front door behind you."

I watched him hurry down the stairs. And I watched the front door slam behind him. A few seconds later I heard the car rumble down the drive.

I went back to my room and pulled a big pile of comic books down from the shelf. I got a big bag of cookies from the kitchen. I took them over to the bed and made myself comfortable.

It was going to be a wonderful day after all.

ABOUT THE AUTHOR

Photograph © Dan Nelken

R.L. (Robert Lawrence) Stine is one of the best-selling children's authors in history. His Goosebumps series, along with such series as Fear Street, The Nightmare Room, Rotten School, and Mostly Ghostly have sold nearly 400 million books in this country alone. And they are translated into 32 languages.

The *Goosebumps* TV series was the top-rated kids' series for three years in a row. R.L.'s TV movies, including *The Haunting Hour: Don't Think About It* and *Mostly Ghostly*, are perennial Halloween favorites. And his scary TV series, *R.L. Stine's The Haunting Hour*, is in its second season on The Hub network.

R.L. continues to turn out Goosebumps books, published by Scholastic. In addition, his first horror novel for adults in many years, titled *Red Rain*, will be published by Touchstone books in October 2012.

R.L. says that he enjoys his job of "scaring kids." But the biggest thrill for him is turning kids on to reading.

R.L. lives in New York City with his wife, Jane, an editor and publisher, and King Charles Spaniel, Minnie. His son, Matthew, is a sound designer and music producer.